The Chalk Boy
© 2009, Joshua Conkel
Trade Edition, 2021
ISBN 978-1-934962-78-7

The Cover: Artwork courtesy of *The Management Company*

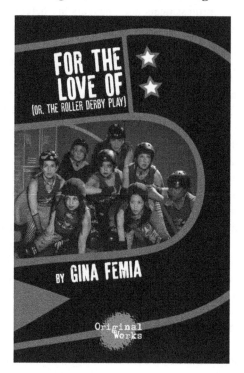

FOR THE LOVE OF (or, The Roller Derby Play)
By Gina Femia

Synopsis: When Joy gets on the Brooklyn Scallywags and meets the star, Lizzie Lightning, she and her long term partner Michelle find their lives turned upside down. *For The Love Of* asks how much you're willing to sacrifice – or lose – in order to follow your heart.

Cast Size: 9 Diverse Females

THE CHALK BOY

By Joshua Conkel

The Chalk Boy opened on September 4th, 2008 in simultaneous productions in New York and Los Angeles. The New York production was produced by The Management at UNDER St. Mark's and had the following cast:

Penelope (Penny) Lauder - Jennifer Harder
Breanna Stark - Kate Huisentruit
Lauren Radley - Mary Catherine Donnelly
Trisha Sorensen - Marguerite French

Directed by Joshua Conkel
Stage Managed by Kelsi Welter

The Los Angeles production was produced by Company of Angels at The Alexandria. The cast was as follows:

Penelope (Penny) Lauder - Sarah Rosenberg
Breanna Stark - Sonora Chase*
Lauren Radley - Amy Golden
Trisha Sorensen - Claire Bocking

Directed by Courtney Sale
Stage Managed by Ricki McKissock

*Jennifer Harder flew to Los Angeles and filled in as Breanna Stark for several of the last performances.

Cast of Characters

PENELOPE (PENNY) LAUDER:
15, maladjusted, melancholy, and on a search for
meaning.

BREANNA STARK:
15, Penny's best friend. Introspective and masculine.
Wears her heart on her sleeve.

LAUREN RADLEY:
15, a nice Christian girl. Also plays MOM, GILL, and
MRS. CHALK.

TRISHA SORENSEN:
15, an athlete and Breanna's best friend.
Also plays MISS MURKOWSKI, JEFF CHALK, and
DOCTOR SALISBURY.

Scene
The playing space is defined by several chalkboards of
varying sizes that are drawn or moved about to suggest
various locations. There should be lots of shadow around
the playing space for the actors to move in and out of.
Also, there may be a small prop table onstage to hold odd
and ends. In general, a few chairs and small props,
coupled with sound design, should indicate setting when
needed. The play is written to be performed without
interruption or blackouts and with actors transforming
onstage whenever possible. Let us not be trapped by
literalism.

Time
Clear Creek, Washington. The present-ish.

THE CHALK BOY

ACT ONE

(As the audience enters the space there is pop music playing. Two teenage girls are drawing on the chalkboards. They occasionally giggle, dance a little, make a comment to one another, but they pay little attention to us. LAUREN RADLEY is a perky girl-next-door in designer jeans. TRISHA SORENSEN, her friend, is in sportswear and a t-shirt that reads, "Christian Athletes". They are drawing feverishly on the chalkboards now, as if a time limit is upon them. They draw houses, pine trees, roads, a school, a football field, a McDonald's, and, finally, a long creek. As the audience is seated and the music comes down, the girls quickly fix their hair and adjust their clothes one last time. Lauren nods to Trisha as if to say, "let's go" and the play begins. They speak directly to the audience.)

LAUREN: Hello. First of all, we want to thank you all for coming to this event. My name is Lauren Radley and this is Trisha Sorensen and we're here representing the Fellowship of Christian Athletes, of which I am the President. Even though I no longer play Volleyball because it conflicts with the Spring musical.

TRISHA: You all look really nice. I hope you enjoyed the Orangeade in the lobby. I made it.

LAUREN: So before we begin, we wanted to start with a prayer, so let's all of us join hands. Go ahead don't be shy. *(Lauren and Trisha link hands and bow their heads.)* Hi, God. It's me, Lauren Radley. I hope you're well. Please look over me and my family as well as Trisha and her family, lord. Please forgive us our trespasses, lord. We care not what we do. Please look over all the awesome people in the world, lord, and take pity on the not-so-awesome. Last of all, please help us to understand recent events and gain wisdom from them, lord. Let us reach catharsis through your love or what have you. Okay, thanks. Bye, God.

TRISHA: Bye. Amen.

LAUREN: *(Back to audience)* Okay, so... we're here to tell you about Clear Creek, Washington and the events that unfolded there.

(Trisha writes, "Clear Creek, WA" on the board. As the presentation continues, Trisha hurriedly tries to point out everything that is being discussed on the chalkboards. It is exhausting.)

LAUREN: This is Clear Creek High School, where we go.

TRISHA: There's our football field. GOOOOOOOO Vikings! And there's our McDonald's.

LAUREN: How do you describe a town like Clear Creek?

TRISHA: It's a shit hole.

LAUREN: Trisha!

TRISHA: Well, it is.

LAUREN: Have you ever been to Disney World? It's totally magical, which is why it's called the magical kingdom. But then you leave Disney World and you're in Orlando. Orlando is not magical. Orlando is strip malls and chain restaurants. Clear Creek is kind of like that, but smaller and in Washington instead of Florida.

TRISHA: And there aren't any beaches.

LAUREN: Right. No beaches. We have a creek though. Clear Creek. Which is sort of a misnomer, really, because it's actually full of cheeseburger wrappers and old tires.

TRISHA: Yeah, I guess it used to be different, like there were all these farms and stuff. My grandma can remember when there were no highways here. She keeps a candy dish of pills on her table and drinks a twelve pack of Bud Light every day so...

LAUREN: One thing that's awesome about Clear Creek is we have every restaurant you could ever imagine. They just opened up a Taco Bell slash Pizza Hut on Piney Street, which was really exciting.

TRISHA: Oh. I forgot to draw Taco Bell.

(Trisha begins to frantically draw it.)

LAUREN: You're embarrassing me.

TRISHA: I wish we were there right now! I want a grilled stuffed burrito!

LAUREN: We'll go after, now shh! *(Trisha freezes. They continue the presentation.)* Anyway, where was I? Oh yeah. Clear Creek is one of *those* towns. You know the ones. They all look exactly alike from the highway at night, forming a dotted line across America's grossly obese belly.

TRISHA: Wow. That's really poetical.

LAUREN: Thanks, Trish. *(To audience)* Clear Creek is where the events you are about to witness took place and it's these events that make Clear Creek a little different than other towns. Beneath its banal exterior, this town hides a nasty secret. Part One. *The Town That Dreaded Sundown.*

(Trisha writes "Part One" on the board and keeps tally marks for the passing days.)

LAUREN & TRISHA: Day one.

TRISHA: No big deal. Probably nobody noticed except for, like, his mom.

LAUREN & TRISHA: Day two.

TRISHA: The police are called.

LAUREN: People start looking. The mall. The woods. Police dogs sniff at the wet grass.

LAUREN & TRISHA: Day five.

TRISHA: By this time it's all over the news. People start to walk quicker on the street.

LAUREN: And lose sleep. I haven't slept.

TRISHA: Me neither.

LAUREN & TRISHA: Day seven.

TRISHA: I heard the football players telling faggot jokes on my way to the girls' locker room. I think they're just trying to forget that they could be next, the chickens.

LAUREN: My mother goes bananas. It's like she thinks that somebody is watching her. She's like Jamie Lee Curtis in her own personal *Halloween*.

TRISHA: Right, like your mother could ever wear high wasted bell bottoms.

LAUREN: I know, right?

LAUREN & TRISHA: Day eight.

LAUREN: Paranoia, paranoia, paranoia. The town is on total lockdown.

TRISHA: So much for our youth group trip to Orcas Island.

LAUREN: We'll start on day eight. This is our English teacher, Miss Murkowski, who we think is a paranoid schizo.

(Lauren looks to Trisha expectantly.)

TRISHA: Um. What?

LAUREN: Do your Murkowski for them.

TRISHA: You do it. You're the actress.

LAUREN: Yes, but your Murkowski is funnier.

TRISHA: I think you're being modest. *(To audience)* Lauren played Emily Webb in last year's production of *Our Town* and she was SO good. You don't even know.

LAUREN: Come on.

TRISHA: Ugh. Fine.

(Trisha procures the ugliest pair of glasses ever made and transforms into MISS MURKOWSKI. Lights shift. We are suddenly in a classroom full of teenage chattering. She addresses her class.)

MISS MURKOWSKI: Eyes here, class. Eyes on me. Okey-dokey. I have a very important announcement to read on behalf of the Sheriff's Department, so listen closely. *(She reads from an invisible piece of paper in her hand.)* In light of recent events all persons under the age of eighteen are to go home immediately after school. *(Groans. Murkowski shushes them.)* No, none of that. This is for your protection. *(Reading)* A strict

10

curfew will be in place from sundown to sun up until further notice. Any persons not adhering to the curfew will be subject to disciplinary action including, but not limited to, a two-hundred dollar fine. The curfew is in effect immediately. Thank you. Sheriff Dick Sparks. Sheriff's Department. Clear Creek County. *(She is finished reading.)* Boys and girls, it is imperative that you be careful out there. These are such dangerous times. As immortal as you might feel, you could be taken just like that. *(Snaps her fingers for emphasis.)* When I was your age I knew a girl, Erica Morielli, and she disappeared. They looked and looked but eventually gave up. She ran away, we told ourselves, girls run away all the time. Two months later they found her in an abandoned freezer. HER FACE HAD BEEN SCRAPED OFF. That's when I learned that these things happen all the time and could happen to any of us. Even me, dear old Miss Murkowski. Why, I could be scooped off the street and thrown into a van. It could happen. Somebody could drive me to a secluded location, like by the old abandoned drive-in off Route 9 perhaps, and they could tie me up and abuse me in more ways than you could possibly imagine. It's a simple fact. I could be abused... sexually. I could be stabbed, starved, frozen, dismembered, thrown into an old well... anything. Ah, but I know how to defend myself. I know a trick. Everybody take out your keys. *(She takes out a set of keys.)* Now, you place a key between two fingers like so. See how sharp and jagged that is? You can use that to gouge out the eyes of an attacker. Now, I want you to shout while you do it. *(She punches at the air and shouts as if in a self-defense class.)* No! *(the teens shout "no" in unison.)* NO! *(Again, the teens echo her.)* NOOOOOOOOOOO! *(Silence. Murkowski recovers.)* That's right, boys and girls. If a stranger ever comes up to you, somebody that makes you feel uncomfortable or lays a hand on you, I want you to pop their eye out. POP! Just like a cork. These are our times, boys and girls. These are our times. *(Beat)* Okey-dokey. Mark Temple will now grace us with his oral presentation on Lord of the Flies. Mark, whenever you're ready.

(The lights go back to normal. Lauren applauds as Trisha removes the glasses and becomes herself.)

LAUREN: That was really good! And scary accurate.

TRISHA: Thanks, Lauren.

LAUREN: Moving on. Ladies and gentlemen, we now have the slight displeasure of introducing you to Penny Lauder and Breanna Stark who are-

TRISHA: Total fucking bitches.

LAUREN: Trisha! Try not to curse so much. You are here representing the Fellowship of Christian Athletes, don't forget.

TRISHA: I'm sorry.

LAUREN: *(To audience)* Trish is just upset because Penny-

TRISHA: Shut up, Lauren!

LAUREN: Okay, fine. Anyway, let's just say these are not the most popular girls in school.

TRISHA: They worship the devil!

LAUREN: So this is Penny. *(Penny appears. Her look is sort of punky promiscuous. She has a backpack.)* Penny is a little white trash and sort of an s-l-u-t, or so I'm told. She doesn't have a dad that I know of but her mom is, like, really young. She teaches my mom's Pilates class at that gym for fat ladies in the mall. *(Breanna appears dressed in baggy boy's clothes. She*

12

has a backpack too.) Breanna's family is sort of loaded, but nobody likes her because people say she's a lesbian.

TRISHA: It's true. We were always on the same soccer team when we were little and that's how I know. Breanna Stark used to be my best friend but then she tried to grab my tit at an eighth grade sleepover.

LAUREN: You never told me that.

TRISHA: It was before we were friends and before I made Christ my personal lord and savior.

LAUREN: Oh. *(To Audience)* Anyway, that's enough exposition. We'll be back in a bit.

TRISHA: Kisses, bitches.

(Lauren and Trisha exit. The lights shift as Penny and Breanna begin their scene. A clearing in the woods at dusk. Each girl holds a bottle of cough syrup in their hands. They are in a stare down.)

PENNY: One, two, three… GO.

(Breanna doesn't move.)

BREANNA: Will this work?

PENNY: Yes, I told you it would, now drink it. God! One, two, three… GO.

(They chug their entire bottles. They gag.)

BREANNA: It's hard to drink. Harder than Vodka.

PENNY: John Stratton said it, like, totally fucked him up. Like he couldn't even walk.

BREANNA: Wow.

PENNY: I know, right?

BREANNA: Should we have done that? I have a quiz tomorrow.

PENNY: What quiz?

BREANNA: In Algebra II.

PENNY: There's no quiz in Algebra II.

BREANNA: Yeah, there is.

PENNY: Shut up. No there isn't.

BREANNA: Yeah, there is. I told you like twenty times.

PENNY: When?

BREANNA: Like twenty times. Plus we have a curfew.

PENNY: Like I give a wet shit about quizzes and curfews.

BREANNA: You should listen to me more often.

PENNY: You should be less boring. You know all the guys at school said they'd never even talk to you if you didn't give oral?

BREANNA: Who said that?

PENNY: Lots of guys.

BREANNA: Which guys?

PENNY: I can't say.

BREANNA: I don't give oral.

PENNY: Yes, huh.

BREANNA: I do not.

PENNY: Do too.

BREANNA: Who?

PENNY: Mark Temple.

BREANNA: Just once.

PENNY: So?

BREANNA: So what?

PENNY: So you give oral, that's what.

BREANNA: Only once!

PENNY: But if you didn't then no guys would talk to you and that's my point. You're boring and sometimes I don't even know why I'm friends with you.

BREANNA: So don't be.

PENNY: Maybe I won't. Maybe I'll go hang out with Trisha Sorensen like you used to.

BREANNA: Go ahead. Everybody would just make fun of you because everybody knows that Trisha pooped her pants at the Hot Springs and wiped her butt with a newspaper.

PENNY: That's just a rumor.

BREANNA: How would you know?

PENNY: Because I'm the one who made it up.

BREANNA: Penny!

PENNY: What? She's a bitch.

BREANNA: You are such a whore.

(Penny gives Breanna a Charlie horse.)

PENNY: Don't ever call me that!

BREANNA: Sorry! God. *(Rubbing the spot.)* That really hurt.

PENNY: I meant it to.

BREANNA: God.

PENNY: Well…

BREANNA: What?

PENNY: You shouldn't have called me that. And stop saying "god' after everything. It's so annoying.

BREANNA: Sorry. *(Beat)* People threw food at her in the cafeteria. We all called her "shit stain."

PENNY: What do you care? I thought you hated her.

BREANNA: I do, but what did Trisha Sorensen ever do to you?

PENNY: Nothing. I don't know. Shut up.

BREANNA: Tell me.

PENNY: Okay, okay. Stop giving me the third degree. God! So remember when you and me and stubby and Trisha and Jeff were at The Olive Garden last Spring?

BREANNA: Uh huh. What?

PENNY: I let Jeff Chalk finger me under the table and-

BREANNA: Oh my god, gross!

PENNY: And I didn't want Trisha to tell anybody! She was the only one who knew.

BREANNA: Penny, I've known her, like, my whole life. She wouldn't tell anybody.

PENNY: Now she won't.

BREANNA: Gross.

PENNY: Shut up, Breanna.

BREANNA: You are nasty.

PENNY: I said shut up!

BREANNA: Fine, jeez. I don't see why you let Jeff do that. Do you like him or something?

PENNY: I don't know.

BREANNA: You deserve better. Somebody who laughs at your jokes. Somebody who likes you for you. *(The cough syrup high kicks in at this precise moment.)* Somebody who likes the way the setting sun bounces off your golden hair. *(Beat)* I feel dizzy.

PENNY: Yeah, well you just drank a whole bottle of cough syrup. Dizzy is the goal, I guess.

BREANNA: I can see everything breathing.

PENNY: You retard.

BREANNA: Why are you so mean to people?

(Penny's high kicks in.)

PENNY: Who knows why anybody does anything?

BREANNA: Do you see that? Everything is breathing.

PENNY: Yeah. Wow! Breanna?

BREANNA: Uh huh?

PENNY: I think we should do it now.

BREANNA: Okay.

PENNY: Do you have the stuff?

BREANNA: Yeah.

PENNY: Then let us begin. *(Something strange is happening with the lights. Eerie music. Penny pulls an ornate dagger from her bag.)* We start by drawing a pentagram in the earth with the sacred dagger. *(She hands the dagger to Breanna who uses it to carve a pentagram into the ground as Penny retrieves five white candles from her own bag. She sees Breanna's work.)* That's a Star of David, dummy. Do it over!

(Breanna erases the circle with her sneaker and quickly draws it again as penny lights each candle and places it at each of the star's points. Breanna unfolds a purple cloth and they kneel on it.)

BREANNA: *(Chanting)* This purple cloth is for protection.

PENNY: This purple cloth is for protection. *(She lights a black candle.)* Visit us, spirits. Bless us with your patronage.

PENNY & BREANNA: With this candle we invoke thee. *(Penny pulls a metal bowl from her bag. Breanna pulls a plastic bag full of garlic from hers.)* We offer you this bowl of garlic.

BREANNA: Speak with us.

(Penny pulls a goblet from her bag. She looks to Breanna.)

PENNY: Did you bring the ceremonial wine? *(Breanna pulls a box of wine from her bag and pours some into the goblet. Penny uses a needle to prick her finger and then squeezes it into the goblet.)* Breanna, give me your finger. *(Breanna timidly offers her finger and lets out a tiny yelp as Penny pricks it. She lets it drip into the goblet.)* Okay. Lie down. *(Breanna lies with her head in Penny's lap. Penny calls to the heavens while the music reaches a crescendo.)* We call the spirit of Jeff Chalk. Speak through this girl, Jeff. If you have left this mortal coil, enter our circle! Speak through this girl, Jeff Chalk! So mote it be! So mote it be! SO MOTE IT BE!

(The music stops. Pause.)

BREANNA: I don't feel good.

PENNY: Be serious.

BREANNA: I am serious. I think I'm gonna barf.

(Breanna crawls to the edge of the stage and vomits.)

PENNY: Idiot. You broke the circle. God!

BREANNA: Sorry. It's all that cough syrup.

PENNY: You can't handle your drugs. The cough syrup was supposed to enhance it.

BREANNA: I'm sorry.

PENNY: This sucks.

BREANNA: We can try again.

PENNY: It's no use. We're not powerful enough. We need four so we can call the corners.

BREANNA: Call the what now?

PENNY: CORNERS. Don't you read any of the books I give you? I swear... You have to call upon the powers of the North, South, East and West. Like in *The Craft*.

BREANNA: Right. *(Pause. Penny turns from Breanna and sulks.)* Penny, you hardly knew him.

PENNY: It seems that way but you don't know everything. Ever since that time at The Olive Garden I just... I love Jeff Chalk. I mean, I think I love him, kind of.

BREANNA: Wow.

PENNY: Right? And now I might not ever... I mean, I might not ever be able to talk to him again. If he ran away he might not come back. And if he's...

BREANNA: Don't.

PENNY: Well, he's been missing for over a week.

BREANNA: Search and Rescue is looking.

PENNY: So? Did they ever find me all those times I ran away? Search and Rescue didn't find me and I was just at Foot Locker. What if he's dead?

BREANNA: You're better off without him. Guys are shit. I hate how girls are supposed to be these, like, flavorless non-people, these meek little things, just so we can be some dude's cum bucket and squirt out his awful babies.

PENNY: You've never been in love.

BREANNA: Maybe I haven't. But anyway, I'll never wear high heels.

PENNY: Don't be stupid. God!

BREANNA: Sorry. What will make you feel better?

PENNY: I don't know. I think my high wore off.

BREANNA: I know what we can do-

PENNY: I'm just gonna go home.

BREANNA: We can go to Albertson's and do whippets!

PENNY: I don't wanna.

BREANNA: Come on.

PENNY: Who are you taking to the Harvest Dance?

(Breanna gives Penny an incredulous look.)

BREANNA: What? I'm not going to that.

PENNY: If Jeff is alive... I mean, do you think if he comes back he'll ask me to the Harvest Dance? You're right. He's alive. Everything is gonna be fine. I'm gonna marry him some day.

BREANNA: It's dark. We should leave.

PENNY: Penelope Chalk...

BREANNA: I'm barfing to death.

PENNY: Mrs. Jeffrey Chalk...

BREANNA: LET'S GO.

PENNY: All right, already. God!

BREANNA: *(As they exit.)* I think you're still high.

(They are gone. Lauren and Trisha enter. They continue their presentation.)

TRISHA: See? Total freak show.

LAUREN: Okay, now I don't want you to think I'm a b.i.t.c.h. because I would never make fun of somebody for being poor, but Penny Lauder lives in one of those manufactured homes they advertise on television.

TRISHA: It's so sordid.

LAUREN: You don't have to be mean.

TRISHA: She makes my skin crawl.

LAUREN: *(While retrieving a pair of sweat pants and a remote control.)* I know. Here. Help me get into these sweat pants. *(Trisha opens the sweat pants and helps Lauren step into them. Lauren puts a scrunchy into her*

22

hair.) Penny's mom always wears sweat pants. Like, always. And her hair is always pulled back into a scrunchy. She'd actually be really pretty if she'd only try. She's really young for a mom. Like, thirty-one or thirty-two. She went to Clear creek High School with my second cousin Rachel who said she was actually really popular.

TRISHA: Who knew?

LAUREN: Here is a picture of what life is like in the Lauder household. Part Two.

(Trisha writes "Part Two" on the board. Dance music and lights shift. We are in the Lauder's living room. Lauren has transformed into MOM, who is furiously doing Pilates before the blue glow of the television. She hears a noise and stops exercising.)

MOM: Hello? *(She turns off the music with the remote control. A floorboard creaks.)* Is somebody there? Penelope is that you? Hello?

(Penny enters with Breanna. Mom is frightened and jumps.)

PENNY: Yes, it's me. God!

MOM: You scared the shit out of me. I almost bludgeoned you with the remote control.

PENNY: Sorry.

MOM: Hello, Breanna. How is your mother?

BREANNA: She's sort of been-

MOM: Penelope, do you know what time it is? What the hell were you thinking?

PENNY: It's just eight.

MOM: There's a curfew. You think I don't know? Let me tell you something, I know everything. I got eyes on the back of my head and ears like a fox so don't you try anything.

BREANNA: Sorry, Mrs. Lauder. We were just doing one of our spells and lost track of time. Won't happen again.

MOM: You see that it doesn't. And I don't like this witch stuff, Penelope, not at all. I told you that already.

PENNY: Wicca is my religion, mother.

MOM: You're a Lutheran and you know it. Witchcraft or whatever is a, I don't know, a hobby.

PENNY: I'm not a Lutheran and neither are you.

MOM: I am so a Lutheran!

PENNY: Oh yeah? When do you ever got to church?

MOM: I go plenty.

PENNY: Like when?

MOM: PLENTY.

PENNY: And when exactly did you decide to become a Lutheran again? When did you have that great epiphany that you should be a Lutheran?

MOM: You think you're *so* cute.

PENNY: Well?

MOM: You know that Grandma and Grandpa are Lutherans and their parents before them. Don't change the subject.

PENNY: I can't remember what the subject is.

MOM: I'll tell you, miss smarty pants. You just waltzed through my front door after curfew when something absolutely bonkers is happening in this town. That's the subject. And what if you'd been caught? Picked up by the police? They'd fine me. Deem meet an unfit mother and take you away maybe. You want that? And don't call me "mother". It's passive aggressive the way you say it and I don't like it. My name is Mom.

PENNY: I'll call you Mom if you call me Penny.

MOM: Fine. Have it your way. But I'll have you know Penelope was married to Odysseus. I mean, she was only a queen for Christ's sake.

PENNY: I know, I know. Jesus! What's for dinner?

MOM: I didn't cook. *(Penny glares at her.)* I was too nervous! You had me biting my nails, girly. Anyway, from the looks of that gut I'd say you've had enough. If I've told you once, I've told you a thousand times. If you don't stop gaining weight no boys will ever ask you out.

PENNY: Mom, please...

MOM: I say these things out of love. Do you want to die alone? Hmm? If you keep eating garbage do you know what will happen? One day you'll put on that special little black dress and you'll take a look at yourself in the mirror and it'll look like you're trash bag full of hamburger meat. I promise you that.

PENNY: Stop nagging, please. I'm hungry and so is Breanna.

MOM: Well, Breanna lives in that great big house up on Hillcrest so I'd bet she's got food there. In a two thousand dollar stainless steel fridge!

BREANNA: *(Quietly.)* They bought it at Sears.

MOM: As for you... microwave some popcorn. NOT the Butter Lover's.

PENNY: Breanna is staying the night here.

MOM: I didn't say she could do that.

PENNY: Please?

BREANNA: If it's okay.

PENNY: You can't send her home in the dark. Kids are dropping like flies.

MOM: That's not funny.

PENNY: I didn't mean it to be.

MOM: That poor boy is out there in the dark somewhere tonight. Think about that.

BREANNA: We're really sad about Jeff.

MOM: Bless your heart. See, Penelope? Why can't you be more like your friend here? At least she knows how to act like a lady.

BREANNA: Wow.

PENNY: Can she stay the night or not?

MOM: I'm sorry, girls, but it's a school night. I'll drive you home, Breanna. I have to go out anyway. I'm all out of Crystal Light. Just let me get cleaned up.

(Lauren, as Mom, exits.)

PENNY: Brown noser.

BREANNA: Stop.

PENNY: Well, you are.

BREANNA: I was being polite. You want her to like me, don't you?

PENNY: Like you, not hump you. She practically gets wet every time you come here.

BREANNA: Gross!

PENNY: Tell me about it.

(Pause)

BREANNA: I don't want to go home.

PENNY: I know. This sucks.

BREANNA: I don't want to be alone. I want to sleep with you. I hear noises at night. A man. When I'm lying in bed I can hear his footsteps in the driveway. Footsteps in the gravel.

PENNY: There's no man in your driveway.

BREANNA: I know what I hear.

PENNY: Look, I wish you could stay too, but you can't. Anyway, we need to think of a way that we can help find Jeff. Like something nobody's thought of.

BREANNA: I don't really think he's alive.

PENNY: What?

BREANNA: I'm sorry, but I don't. I was trying to make you feel better, but I don't believe it. Not anymore.

PENNY: God, Breanna!

BREANNA: Well, you know what happens to people who disappear around here just as well as I do.

PENNY: Shut up.

BREANNA: Are you mad?

PENNY: Yes.

BREANNA: Do you hate me?

PENNY: Yes.

BREANNA: I'm sorry.

PENNY: It's fine.

BREANNA: Maybe I'm wrong and he's okay.

PENNY: No. You don't get to do that. You don't get to take things back when you upset somebody.

BREANNA: Okay. Then I think Jeff Chalk is dead. I think something really shitty happened to him and now he's dead. Happy? Man, I let you walk all over me and I never say anything just because I want you to like me, or whatever.

PENNY: Dumb bitch.

(Lauren, as Mom, enters with her car keys.)

MOM: Okay. Let's go. Penelope, I want you to lock the doors behind us, all right?

PENNY: Okay.

MOM: And I want your homework started by the time I get back. Do you understand? *(Penny and Breanna are locking eyes.)* Look at me. HEY! Grades are important. I don't want you to ruin your life the way I ruined mine.

PENNY: Okay, okay.

MOM: I'll be back in a half an hour. Love you! *(Lauren, as Mom, exits.)*

PENNY: *(Quietly.)* Get. Out. Of. My. House.

(Breanna sheepishly leaves. Penny paces back and forth slowly thinking.)

PENNY: Mrs. Chalk. Mrs. Penelope Chalk. Penelope Louis Chalk. Penelope Lauder Chalk.

(She continues to pace and talk to herself as Trisha enters and observes her. Penny doesn't see her.)

TRISHA: *(To audience.)* Charming. *(During the next few lines she sets up for the next scene, placing a television and chair. She puts on a men's track jacket and baseball cap, but does not transform.)* So this is sort of a sub section of Part Two. Let's call it Part Two A. *(She adds an 'A' next to where "Part Two" is written.)* Around this time it's pretty common for us girls to sleep over at each others houses in big groups. Even on school nights. Not because we're all bull dykes like Breanna Stark, but because it just feels safer. Fun fact. The noise that Breanna heard was actually her own

29

eyelashes brushing against her pillow case and not a man's footsteps in the gravel like she thought. She never figured that one out. I know this because I'm the narrator and I'm whatchamacallit... omniscient. *(She sits down in the chair with the television in her lap.)* Anyways, this is the dream that Penny had that night.

(LIGHTS SHIFT TO: We are somewhere dark and surreal. Strange noises drift quietly from the shadows. Trisha has transformed into JEFF CHALK. Jeff Chalk sits in the chair with the television in his lap. He dully flips through the channels, transfixed. Penny, who has been pacing through all of this, notices him.)

PENNY: Jeff?

JEFF CHALK: I can't get ESPN down here. It totally sucks.

PENNY: Where are we?

JEFF CHALK: A hole. A basement?

PENNY: Are you hurt? Something is different about you.

JEFF CHALK: I'm bored. I've been spending most of my days asleep. Waiting for something to happen. Nothing ever happens around here. I guess this is something though, isn't it?

PENNY: I don't understand. Is someone holding you here or--

JEFF CHALK: He gave me this TV to watch. No cable though. I've been watching a lot of *M.A.S.H.* That shit is always on.

PENNY: You know, you're more popular than ever. Suddenly everybody thinks you're like the greatest guy who ever lived. I got called into the principal's office to talk to the police. They don't have a fucking clue.

JEFF CHALK: I'm kind of lucky when you think about it. When I get out of here I'll be like a total celebrity. In the papers and shit.

PENNY: You're already in the papers. Listen, I was wondering... do you like me?

JEFF CHALK: You seem sad a lot of the time.

PENNY: I am. Aren't you?

JEFF CHALK: Not really. Wanna watch *The Price is Right*?

PENNY: Sure. *(She watches television with him.)* When it happened the first time I couldn't tell if you really liked me at all. I'm still not sure.

JEFF CHALK: Ssh.

PENNY: What you did, I've never let anybody do that to me. And I really like it when we meet by the creek but I don't know why we have to keep it a secret.

JEFF CHALK: This dude comes down here sometimes. He's okay. At first I thought this was all some kind of gay thing because he asks to touch my face all the time. That's it. Just touch my face. I thought it was creepy at first, but now I'm used to it. I mean, as long as he doesn't do anything else. It's funny, I'm so used to being told what to do. I guess I was used to it. Down here though... I mean, at least he asks me first. The guy loves me. Not in a gay way. I think he's just lonely. Anyway, he gets me whatever I want as long as I let him touch my face and I talk to him when he wants, and like that. *(He smacks the side of the television.)* I'm thinking of asking for cable. Man, it's gonna be awesome when I go back. Things will be different because I'm different. Something different finally happened to me.

PENNY: I wish you'd touch me like that. I'd like it.

JEFF CHALK: I'm watching my show.

PENNY: Come back with me.

JEFF CHALK: I can't. Everything is gonna be different now.

(Penny exits. LIGHTS SHIFT TO: Trisha gets out of Jeff drag as Lauren enters and joins her. They continue speaking to the audience.)

LAUREN: So here's the 411 on Jeff Chalk. He's not especially smart.

TRISHA: Or very interesting.

LAUREN: He's athletic.

TRISHA: He's all body.

LAUREN: Yeah. That body is... wow.

TRISHA: He's cute.

LAUREN: He's gorgeous.

TRISHA: Tell them about the horse girls.

LAUREN: There are these girls at school we call the horse girls. They're girls who live on farms, usually. They have greasy hair and Target jeans and are really quiet. Thing is, they all love horses. They sit there and draw horses in their notebook all day long, never talking to anybody.

TRISHA: There's five or six of them. Kelly Sanders is one.

LAUREN: I'm secretly kind of one of them. I mean, I love horses. My grandparents have this ranch in California. It's amazing there. When I was twelve I fell in love with this horse named Foggy. I'd, like, groom him and ride him and whisper all my stupid secrets to him. I felt so close to him, even though he was sort of quiet and aloof as horses tend to be. He was my best friend that summer, which must sound totally queer.

TRISHA: Horses are a metaphor! *(Lauren glares at her.)* Sorry. Sheesh.

LAUREN: Anyway, one day I was leading Foggy through a field when I slipped in mud and fell. It was quick as lighting and I guess the impact of my little body hitting the dirt must have spooked him. He reared up his front legs and came down on me. Hard. His hoof hit me right on the ear. And I was wearing these really cute earrings I got for my birthday too. It was shocking because I'd trusted him so much, you know? I was like, F you, Foggy! I didn't go near him for the rest of the summer. But I wanted to. Because he was so beautiful. And the fact that he was all aloof and dangerous made me want to be near him even more. And, really, that is sort of how Jeff Chalk is.

TRISHA: He's also a shoe-in for Prom King in a couple of years.

LAUREN: Oh, and also, this one time, Jeff got a bloody nose in P.E. when Stubby hit him in the face with a volleyball and I saw Penny Lauder pick up the bloody tissue and put it in her pocket.

TRISHA: You lie.

LAUREN: For real.

TRISHA: What did you do?

LAUREN: Nothing, but it was really weird. I was P.O.'d at her. Like, really mad.

TRISHA: What she did was vomit worthy.

LAUREN: No, actually. Because I didn't want her to have it.

TRISHA: I'm dying. This is a train wreck.

LAUREN: Let's move on. Day twelve. Part Three.

(Trisha brings the tally on the board to twelve as-- LIGHTS SHIFT. BOOTY SHAKING MUSIC AS: Lauren and Trisha are dancing like women in a hip hop video, much too suggestively for girls their age.)

TRISHA: The Harvest dance, bitches!

LAUREN: Trisha! No cursing! Oh! And Penny and Breanna are friends again. That's just how it is here. Go with it.

(The music fades into a slow jam as Trisha and Lauren fade into the dark corners in the background. On either side of the stage's rear, they slow dance with their backs turned to the audience. Their arms are crossed over their breasts and their hands caress their backs, creating the illusion they are each a couple slow dancing. Penny and Breanna enter and awkwardly sway back and forth to the music.)

BREANNA: Some dance. What kind of dance ends at 4:30 in the afternoon anyway?

PENNY: I love the theme. "Under the Sea". Ha!

BREANNA: Yeah, these butcher paper starfish make me feel like a mermaid.

PENNY: Look at Ashley.

BREANNA: Just because she's got huge jugs she thinks she's better than everybody.

PENNY: I would never wear that dress. What a skank.

BREANNA: I know. You could get hepatitis just from looking. I can't stand her.

PENNY: Me neither. Wait, who is she dancing with? Is that--

BREANNA: It's John Stratton. I thought he liked you. Guess not.

PENNY: Whatever. I don't care.

BREANNA: Me neither. Why are we here, anyway? I'd rather be doing, like, anything.

PENNY: I know, right? I wish Jeff were here.

BREANNA: I know.

PENNY: I had a dream about him, you know. I dream about him all the time now.

BREANNA: That's messed up.

PENNY: Do you think he would ask me to dance? If he were here, I mean?

BREANNA: You'd probably have to ask him. Guys suck that way.

PENNY: I think he would.

BREANNA: Maybe. We should cast a spell to make Ashley's breasts fall off.

PENNY: We can't do that. It would come back to us three times fold.

BREANNA: I know. It would just be fun, is all. Anyway, I know you and Jeff had some sort of... connection. But I think you're only hung up on him because he's gone now and the whole town's obsessed with him.

PENNY: That's not it. Anyway, why not obsess over him? He is the most popular guy in school.

BREANNA: Since when does that matter to you?

PENNY: I don't know. It's just... why does it have to be just *us* all the time, you know?

BREANNA: Oh.

PENNY: No, I mean, you're my best friend. But there are other people in the world besides just us.

BREANNA: Yeah, but we hate them.

PENNY: Yeah, but what if we don't have to. Seriously, sometimes it just feels like this whole town is just me and you and, like, two other people. Maybe we should broaden our horizons.

BREANNA: I don't want to. We both grew up here. We have fifteen years of experience that says we're better than them. We're getting out of here. Just look at how powerful our magic has gotten in the past six months.

PENNY: What magic? Nothing ever works.

BREANNA: You're so cynical.

PENNY: Whatever.

BREANNA: Seriously, Penny, I think you're really special. I think there's this sweet, sensitive, gorgeous person inside of you that nobody notices. But I notice. I just wanted you to know.

PENNY: Wow. Thank you.

BREANNA: I'm serious. I wish you saw yourself the way that I see you. *(Pause)* Quiet! Here comes Trisha Sorensen.

(Trisha dances downstage from her shadowy corner.)

TRISHA: What's up, ladies?

PENNY & BREANNA: Hey, Trisha.

TRISHA: Some dance, huh?

BREANNA: Yeah, it's awesome.

TRISHA: Have you guys seen Mark Temple?

BREANNA: No. Thank God.

TRISHA: Oh, right. I forgot you gave him a BJ.

BREANNA: I did not!

TRISHA: Oh. I'm sorry. Was I not supposed to know that? Well, I know a lot, Breanna Stark.

PENNY: Leave us alone.

TRISHA: I'm not doing anything. Anyway, if you see Mark tell him I'm looking for him. I think he's avoiding me.

BREANNA: I can't imagine why.

TRISHA: Hey...

BREANNA: Hey what?

TRISHA: You didn't happen to hear a rumor about me, did you?

BREANNA: No, not at all.

TRISHA: Whatever. I'm gonna go find Mark. Kisses, bitches.

(Trisha retreats to her shadowy corner and continues to impersonate a slow dancing couple.)

BREANNA: I hate her.

PENNY: You and everybody else.

BREANNA: Let's hit the snack table. I want some calamari.

PENNY: I'm not allowed.

BREANNA: You're not fat.

PENNY: Tell that to my mom.

BREANNA: She hates fat.

PENNY: I know. God! It's like she's pushing me to purge.

BREANNA: Well, do you want to dance?

PENNY: What? With you?

BREANNA: Sure.

PENNY: We can't do that. What would people say?

BREANNA: What do you mean? Lots of girls are dancing together.

PENNY: *(Looking around.)* Okay, I guess. *(They begin to awkwardly slow dance.)* I'm glad we're friends again.

BREANNA: Me too. Let's never fight again.

(Breanna lays her head on Penny's shoulder. They slow dance for a minute. Lauren approaches them.)

LAUREN: Hi, guys.

PENNY & BREANNA: Hi Lauren.

LAUREN: It's weird that Jeff's not here, isn't it?

PENNY: Yeah.

LAUREN: I kind of wanted him to ask me, but...

PENNY: I think a lot of girls did.

LAUREN: Yeah, well. Anyway, I want to ask you something. This is kind of awkward. Did either of you spread a rumor that Trisha had an accident in her pants?

PENNY: What? No.

LAUREN: No, I know. That's what I told her too, but... she thinks you did it, Breanna.

BREANNA: Me?

LAUREN: Because you're not friends anymore. Her feelings are really hurt. I mean, she's actually really sensitive.

39

BREANNA: Right.

LAUREN: Can I ask you guys another question? You don't have to answer.

PENNY: Okay.

LAUREN: Are you guys really witches?

PENNY: Yeah.

LAUREN: Oh. Well, I want you to know that you're always welcome at youth group. It's really fun. We meet at the flagpole in the lawn every morning if you ever---

BREANNA: Thanks. *(To Penny.)* Let's go.

PENNY: Okay.

LAUREN: Anyway, bye. Have fun!

(Penny and Breanna exit. Trisha approaches Lauren.)

TRISHA: Why were you just talking to Breanna and Penny?

LAUREN: I wasn't.

TRISHA: Then what the fuck was that I just saw? I thought I told you not to talk to them.

LAUREN: Who are you cursing at right now? Seriously, it must be someone else.

TRISHA: You're supposed to be *my* friend.

LAUREN: I am.

TRISHA: Then why were you just chatting it up with that carpet muncher and that trailer trash?

LAUREN: Look, I was just trying to find out if they were the ones who spread that rumor about you.

TRISHA: I already know that they were.

LAUREN: How?

TRISHA: Because Emily Grey, from my Lacrosse team, told me that Penny told her. I told you that already. Man, I'm gonna kick Penny Lauder's ass!

LAUREN: Did it ever occur to you that people wouldn't spread rumors about you if you were a little nicer to them?

TRISHA: I AM NICE. I mean, I try to be nice but some people make it really hard. They're such freak shows! Especially Breanna. God, I hate her! It's like, she knows this person who *used* to be me, but isn't me anymore. You know? I wanna be like, *you don't know my fuckin' life, bitch!*

LAUREN: I think they're kind of interesting.

TRISHA: What? I'm gagging.

LAUREN: I know they're going to hell and everything, but at least they don't care what anybody thinks of them. That's more than I can say for some people around here.

TRISHA: Fine. Hang out with them. Sacrifice cats. See if I care. I'm gonna go find Mark.

(Trisha exits. Lauren looks to the audience.)

LAUREN: That's terrific. You try to help somebody and they poop on you. Anyway, Part Three, I guess. Day fourteen. Two weeks in.

(She brings the tally on the chalkboard to fourteen and writes "Part Three". LIGHTS SHIFT. CREEPY MUSIC... Behind the football field Penny and Breanna play with a Ouija board.)

BREANNA: Stop moving it.

PENNY: I'm not moving it.

BREANNA: Well, I'm not moving it.

PENNY: I know. *(Suddenly putting on her mysterious voice.)* It's the spirits. They're all around us, called upon by our magicks.

BREANNA: Creepy.

PENNY: Do not fear the spirits, Breanna.

BREANNA: Okay.

PENNY: Now ask your question.

BREANNA: Now? Just, like, ask?

PENNY: Ask.

BREANNA: Okay. Um... spirits? Does John Stratton like Penny--

PENNY: Breanna!

BREANNA: -- Because he was dancing with Ashley.

PENNY: You can't ask the spirits that! God!

BREANNA: Why not?

PENNY: Because it's totally trivial, is why.

BREANNA: It's not trivial to me.

PENNY: Ask them something else.

BREANNA: Fine. *(Pause.)* I can't think of anything.

PENNY: Let me. *(Mysterious voice.)* Spirit world, tell me... is Jeff Chalk still alive.

(As the indicator begins to move they read its answers in unison. The lights dim. Music.)

PENNY & BREANNA: Yes.

PENNY: Did he run away?

PENNY & BREANNA: No.

BREANNA: Was he abducted?

PENNY & BREANNA: Yes.

PENNY: Where is he now?

PENNY & BREANNA: U-N-D-E-R-G-R-O-U-N-D. Underground.

BREANNA: Buried?

PENNY & BREANNA: No.

PENNY: In a cellar?

PENNY & BREANNA: Yes.

PENNY: Will somebody find him?

PENNY & BREANNA: Yes.

PENNY: When?

PENNY & BREANNA: S-O-O-N. Soon.

PENNY: Soon? Soon, *when*?

PENNY & BREANNA: S-O-O-N.

PENNY: When the fuck is soon? Today?

PENNY & BREANNA: Yes.

PENNY: Is he okay? *(The indicator begins to spin around on the board furiously, not landing on anything.)* IS HE OKAY?

BREANNA: Penny...

PENNY: I said, is he okay?

(The indicator lands on "goodbye".)

BREANNA: Goodbye. Shit, Penny. That was really creepy.

PENNY: Oh my god. Jeff is alive.

BREANNA: Penny--

PENNY: My dream wasn't a dream. It was a prophecy.

BREANNA: Prophecy?

PENNY: Like when you see the future?

BREANNA: I know what it means.

PENNY: Don't you see? This means our magic is getting stronger.

BREANNA: Quiet. Here comes Trisha Sorensen.

(Trisha enters with Lauren behind her.)

TRISHA: Well, well, well. If it isn't he bitches of Eastwick. Sacrificing cats?

LAUREN: Trisha...

TRISHA: *(To Lauren.)* Quiet, you.

BREANNA: What do you want, Trisha?

TRISHA: Nothing. I just thought I smelled cheap hair product out here. Now I know why.

BREANNA: Just leave us alone.

TRISHA: I'm not bothering anyone. Am I bothering anyone, Lauren? *(Lauren opens her mouth to respond but Trisha cuts her off when she notices Penny sitting pensively.)* Why is she being so quiet?

BREANNA: Lauren, get her away from us, please.

TRISHA: *(To Penny.)* I know it was you who started that rumor about me. I just want you to know I plan on telling everybody about Jeff Chalk and the Olive Garden. I mean *everybody*.

BREANNA: You tell anybody that and I'll beat the shit out of you.

TRISHA: Excuse me?

BREANNA: You heard me.

TRISHA: Protecting your pig dyke girlfriend? You want to fight me?

BREANNA: That's what I said.

TRISHA: I'd like to see you try, hag.

BREANNA: Bitch.

TRISHA: LESBO. God, what happened to you? You used to be normal. I can't believe I was ever friends with you. Consider your membership to the secret society of super awesome sisterhood officially revoked.

BREANNA: I don't care.

TRISHA: WE TOOK A BLOOD OATH.

(Penny comes between them.)

PENNY: You know what? I'm sorry. I started that rumor and I shouldn't have so... I'm sorry.

TRISHA: What?

PENNY: Yeah, I was scared you would tell people about Jeff and I guess I just sort of freaked out. I'm sorry. Friends?

LAUREN: See, she apologized Trisha. Let's just go now.

TRISHA: *(To Penny.)* What are you trying to do?

PENNY: Nothing. I'm just apologizing.

TRISHA: You're up to something. I can tell.

PENNY: I'm being sincere. I swear.

LAUREN: *(Placating Trisha.)* See, that's nice. *(To Penny.)* Apology accepted, Penny.

TRISHA: Will you just shut the fuck up, Lauren? You're always *blah, blah, blah* and I'm sick of it. You think you're so much better than everybody else.

LAUREN: No I don't! I... you know what? No. That's it. I can't help you anymore, Trisha. God knows I've tried, but I just... You're a heathen, plain and simple. AND EVEN JESUS HAD LIMITS. I'm leaving.

(Lauren exits. Trisha calls after her.)

TRISHA: Good riddance! *(Back to Penny.)* You think you're so cool. I don't know what Jeff saw in you.

PENNY: Jeff?

TRISHA: Jeff. *Jeff,* Jeff. He told me he was going to ask you out.

BREANNA: You're an asshole.

TRISHA: I'm totally one-hundred percent serious. That was before he disappeared, of course. Poor Penelope Lauder. The one boy who liked her disappeared and then she spent the rest of her life alone with her cats and her Satanism and her pig dyke life partner.

BREANNA: Shut up, shit stain!

PENNY: Jeff was going to ask me out?

TRISHA: Maybe he was and maybe he wasn't.

PENNY: Was he?

BREANNA: Get out of here, Trisha.

47

TRISHA: No!

(Breanna grabs her by the hair and yanks her as hard as she can. She does not let go.)

BREANNA: I said... Get. Out. Of. Here.

(Breanna throws Trisha to the ground, releasing her.)

TRISHA: You're gonna be sorry you did that. Just wait until you hear what I just heard, you stupid bitch!

(Trisha retreats into the shadows, where she begins to transition.)

BREANNA: What a fucking asshole.

PENNY: I don't feel good.

BREANNA: Penny, what's wrong?

PENNY: I have a funny feeling, I guess.

BREANNA: What kind of feeling?

(Trisha suddenly reenters the light as MISS MURKOWSKI.)

MISS MURKOWSKI: Penelope! Breanna! What did you do to Trisha Sorensen? I just saw her crying!

BREANNA: Nothing, she--

MISS MURKOWSKI: -- Never mind that now. Come with me into the gym. Something has happened.

(LIGHTS SHIFT AND... We are in the gym. Anxious chatting fills the air.)

MISS MURKOWSKI: Okey-dokey. Listen up, boys and girls. Eyes here. Eyes on me. *(The chattering doesn't stop so she blows into a whistle. It stops immediately.)* Listen to me. I hate to be the bearer of bad news. There's been a break in the Jeffrey Chalk case. I want you all to be on guard. Mrs. Chalk was collecting her mail, when...

(Lauren, as Mrs. Chalk has appeared in a bubble of light. She is dressed in a bath robe and holds a manila envelope. She opens the envelope and peers inside. She screams. She puts her hand in the envelope and slowly lifts its contents. It is a human finger. She faints. Her light goes out.)

MISS MURKOWSKI: Police and search parties will continue to look for the rest of Jeffrey, but I regret to inform you he is presumed dead. *(Strangely, Miss Murkowski begins to speak in gibberish.)* Blah blah blobbity-blah. Blah blah blah... blah. *(In the meantime,)* blah blah blobbity-blah...

(Miss Murkowski's gibberish begins to fade out until-- LIGHT SHIFT...In the car. Lauren, as Mom, drives Penny and Breanna home. She is in a panic.)

MOM: Right here in our own town! Breanna, I want you to try calling your parents again as soon as we get to the house.

BREANNA: I just don't know where they could be. I hope they didn't go away for the weekend without telling me again.

MOM: They wouldn't do that, sweetie.

BREANNA: Sure they would. They do it all the time. They go to, like, conventions.

MOM: I went to a science fiction convention with my sister last year. She just loves *Star Trek*.

BREANNA: Yeah, not that kind of convention.

PENNY: Breanna's parents are swingers.

MOM: Penelope!

PENNY: What? It's true.

MOM: That is not true. Is that true, Brenna?

BREANNA: Yes.

MOM: Rich people are crazy.

PENNY: Mother!

MOM: I'm sorry. I'm sorry, Breanna. I'm just a little anxious. I need a Valium or something.

PENNY: At your stress level a person needs black tar heroin.

MOM: PENNY. Do you understand what's happened? Right here in our own town? You girls don't know how lucky you are to be young and healthy. Each day of life is a gift. It's a cliché, but it's true. *(To Penny.)* And you! You were a blue baby, Penelope, blue as a damn Smurf and you almost died.

PENNY: Please don't tell this story. It's so gay.

MOM: Penelope!

PENNY: What? God!

MOM: You're cousin Seamus is a gay and I don't think he'd like to hear you talk that way.

PENNY: What guy would sleep with Seamus? He has a birthmark on his face that makes him look like a burn victim.

MOM: Well, I don't like it.

PENNY: Just please don't tell the story. I feel awful

BREANNA: I'd like to hear it.

PENNY: God!

MOM: You were blue. I don't know what causes it, something to do with nitrates in the blood or some such thing, but you sure were blue which apparently is really bad in infants. Not to mention your umbilical cord was strangling you as you emerged from the womb... blah blah blobbity blah...*(Her language begins to devolve into gibberish as something strange happens to the lights. Penny stares out her window.)* Blah blah blobbity blah blah blah…

(Slowly, as if in a dream, Trisha appears in a bubble of light as Jeff Chalk. She is missing a finger. She waves at Penny slowly. Penny, confused, waves back. Trisha as Jeff Chalk disappears as the lights go back to normal.)

MOM: Blobbity blah blah blah. So, yeah, you're lucky to be alive, Miss Tough Stuff. And I'm lucky too.

BREANNA: That is such a sweet story.

MOM: Bless your little heart.

PENNY: I don't feel good.

MOM: What's wrong? Did you eat too much at school?

PENNY: I'm gonna be sick.

MOM: What?

BREANNA: Oh my god.

PENNY: Pull over.

(The car stops. Penny gets out and runs to the edge of the stage and vomits. Mom calls to her.)

MOM: Are you okay, honey? *(Penny wipes her mouth but doesn't answer.)* Penelope?

PENNY: Yes, I'm fine.

(Penny gets back into the car.)

MOM: Do you want to lie down in the back seat?

PENNY: I said I was fine. Just drive. God! *(Mom starts the engine. They drive in silence for a ways.)* I'm gonna have a baby.

(Mom and Breanna stare at her.)

MOM: What did you just say?

PENNY: I'm having Jeff Chalk's baby. I don't want to talk about it.

(Silence. Trisha enters and speaks to the audience.)

TRISHA: Go have some Orangeade. Come back in ten minutes.

(LIGHTS FADE OUT.)

END OF ACT ONE

ACT TWO

(Lauren and Trisha continue their presentation.)

LAUREN: Welcome back.

TRISHA: Hi. Hello.

LAUREN: Is everybody comfortable?

TRISHA: Did you have some Orangeade?

LAUREN: Awesome. Let's start. This is twenty days in now. *(Trisha brings the tally on the board to twenty.)* Complete and utter chaos. Everywhere you go it's strangely quiet, but you can feel terror just beneath. It's weird, Jeff Chalk was just plain old Jeff Chalk from school, and now... Now he is a local obsession. Not just for us, for everybody. Part Four. *(Trisha writes "Part Four" on the board.)* Ready, Trisha?

TRISHA: Yep.

LAUREN: Ready, set, go.

(Lauren exits as Penny enters and-- LIGHTS SHIFT TO... The same clearing from Act One. Penny and Trisha stand facing one another. Trisha has a bottle of cough syrup.)

PENNY: One, two, three... GO!

(Trisha chugs it.)

TRISHA: Sick!

PENNY: It totally works though. You get so fucked up.

TRISHA: Really?

PENNY: Absolutely. I would do some too, but the baby and all...

TRISHA: Yeah. You know, I was at Old Navy and they had the cutest baby clothes. They had this pink hoodie that says "hot stuff" in rhinestones, only it's for a baby!

PENNY: Wow.

TRISHA: We should totally go.

PENNY: Okay.

TRISHA: Oh my god, I'm glad we're friends now. Lauren never does anything like this. We probably would've been friends sooner if you weren't spending so much time with that lesbian pig, Breanna Stark.

PENNY: She won't get off my tit. Every time I turn around she's there begging for my attention. People ask me if I'm afraid to have a baby and I tell them I already have one.

TRISHA: She probably has a big crush on you. Breanna Stark is a dyke. Everybody knows that.

PENNY: She's okay. She's just freaked out by everything that's been happening.

TRISHA: Mark Temple said she gave, like, the worst head ever. She must be a dyke.

PENNY: So? I think it's okay to be gay as long as you, like, keep it to yourself.

TRISHA: Gross.

PENNY: Anyway, I don't have time to coddle her. I've got my own shit to deal with, you know? They haven't

54

found Jeff yet. Just his finger. I wonder what he would say. Do you think he'd be happy or do you think he'd want to get rid of it?

TRISHA: Men hate babies.

PENNY: That's not true.

TRISHA: Oh yeah? Where's your father? Where's mine? Face it. Men hate babies.

PENNY: Still. I'd like to find him and tell him. I never told anybody this, but before he was gone we would meet in secret sometimes. Down by the creek. We didn't talk much though. We mostly just kissed. He was a really wet kisser. I had to wipe my face with my sleeve. Sometimes it was more than that. He'd put his finger in me or I'd give him a BJ... But all that time, every time we were together, he never gave me any indication as to how he really felt about me. If he just would've touched me in a certain way, just maybe touched my face in a gentle way, I would have known. No such luck.

TRISHA: Guys never tell you how they really feel. They're pricks that way.

PENNY: I guess.

TRISHA: I feel weird.

PENNY: I wonder if there's a way I can communicate with him...

TRISHA: Penny?

PENNY: By magic, I mean.

TRISHA: I feel bad.

PENNY: I'll consult my book of shadows. *(Trisha groans and crawls away from Penny.)* Are you even listening to me?

TRISHA: I feel dizzy.

PENNY: Of course you do. That's supposed to happen. But does it feel good?

TRISHA: No.

PENNY: Pay attention to your body. How does it feel?

TRISHA: I guess it feels good.

PENNY: Yeah?

TRISHA: Yeah. It feels good.

PENNY: Good.

(Lauren enters.)

LAUREN: What are you guys doing here?

TRISHA: What are *you* doing here?

LAUREN: I come here to study sometimes. What happened to you, Trisha? You look awful.

TRISHA: I'm fucking trippin'!

LAUREN: You drank cough syrup? *(Trisha laughs uncontrollably.)* Awesome. That's brilliant, Trish. Next I suppose you'll become a meth head.

PENNY: Don't overreact. It's no big deal.

LAUREN: I'm not overreacting!

PENNY: What, you never get high?

LAUREN: No, actually, I want to go to Stanford so I try not to be totally bombed all the time.

TRISHA: DON'T JUDGE ME.

PENNY: I know! God!

LAUREN: Penny, are you high too?

PENNY: No. I'm pregnant.

LAUREN: That's why I was asking. I'd have to tell the authorities if I thought you were in danger of hurting your unborn baby.

PENNY: Shut the fuck up, Lauren.

TRISHA: Yeah. Leave us alone.

LAUREN: I have to go, anyway. I'm memorizing my lines for the play. I got the lead. We're doing *Wit.*

(Lauren exits.)

PENNY: Bitch.

TRISHA: She's just jealous because she liked Jeff.

PENNY: Her?

TRISHA: Didn't you know?

PENNY: No.

TRISHA: I thought everybody knew that. Hey, who do you think the most popular boy is now that Jeff is dead?

PENNY: Nobody knows if Jeff is dead.

TRISHA: Sorry. *Probably* dead, then.

PENNY: I don't know. Mark Temple?

TRISHA: I think so too!

PENNY: Trisha, let's do a spell.

TRISHA: I can't. I'm a Christian.

PENNY: No, you aren't.

TRISHA: Well, I'm trying to be but I'm having a crisis of faith or something. Turns out it's a lot harder than I thought. There's a lot of rules to learn. Things I'm not supposed to do.

PENNY: You don't have to participate. You can just be my helper.

TRISHA: Uh, okay. What sort of spell should we do?

PENNY: Well, I found this protection spell for pregnancy and I sort of want to try it.

TRISHA: I feel like shit, Penny.

PENNY: Do you want to help or not?

TRISHA: Okay, okay.

PENNY: I mean, it's not all that involved or anything. It's just a precaution, is all.

TRISHA: Against what?

PENNY: Well, it's like, what if everything that's been happening around here, everything negative, what if it could, like, effect the baby? What if the baby was born sad? Like I was.

TRISHA: That's stupid. People aren't born sad.

PENNY: I think I was. Have you ever noticed that some people have, like, an essential quality? Sadness or happiness or anger or whatever. On the happiest day of my life, I think you'd still be able to sense a little hint of sadness, just under the surface. Like it's always there.

TRISHA: I think I was born pissed off. Maybe it's hormonal, but most of the time I just want to punch people in the face.

PENNY: Anyway, I don't want to pass that on.

TRISHA: Okay, okay. What do we do?

(Penny rummages through her bag and retrieves an apple, a dagger and a green candle. She passes the candle to Trisha.)

PENNY: Here. Light this.

(Trisha lights the candle. Penny cuts the apple in half.)

TRISHA: This candle smells like Pine-Sol.

PENNY: Pine is for fertility. The green is for luck. Okay, come over here. *(Trisha comes closer to Penny.)* I'm going to lay me head in your lap. *(Penny hands half of the apple to Trisha.)* You rub this on my belly and while you do it imagine that all the negative energy from inside me is getting sucked into the apple. All of the sadness, all of the fear, into the apple... *(Penny lifts her shirt and Trisha rubs the apple on her bare tummy. It is quiet for a long time.)*

TRISHA: I feel *so* gay right now.

PENNY: Ssh. Okay, that's good. Now bury that half somewhere. *(Trisha searches for a good place to bury the apple.)* Now I fill the other half with my positivity and all my hopes for the future. *(She closes her eyes tightly and "fills" the fruit.)* And I eat it. *(She takes a bite and is quiet for a moment.)* Okay. I feel a lot better about things now.

TRISHA: *(Holding her tummy, trying not to be sick.)* Great. That's awesome.

PENNY: Blessed be!

TRISHA: Yeah. Blessed be. Whatever that means.

(LIGHTS SHIFT. EERIE MUSIC AS... Penny exits as Trisha turns to the audience.)

TRISHA: The night of the twenty-second day. Part Five.

(Trisha updates the figures on the board and exits. Breanna appears in a bubble of light. A candle burns as she pours powders and liquids into a mortar and pestol. She stirs and chants.)

BREANNA: I stir, I change, I manifest. Penelope's love that suits me best. I stir, I change, I manifest, Penelope's love that suits me best. I stir, I change, I manifest, Penelope's love that suits me best.

(She continues to chant sotto voce as Lauren appears in a separate bubble of light somewhere else. She is praying.)

LAUREN: Dear God. Hi. It's me, Lauren Radley. I hope you're well. I'm fine. Okay, I'm not really fine, that's an overstatement. I'm trying to understand your plan for me. For all of us. You have one, right? No, I know you do. It's just that sometimes the world seems like it's an

60

orderless place where nothing ever happens for a reason, and that the best we can hope for is to hunker down and hope for good luck. But I know that can't be the case, right? Of course not. You have a plan for me. Just, please lord, help me understand what it might be. Love, Lauren Radley.

(Lauren's bubble pops out. Penny appears in Breanna's bubble. She is naked and wrapped in a sheet.)

BREANNA: I stir, I change, I manifest, Penelope's love that suits me best...

PENNY: Breanna? *(Breanna is still chanting.)* It's the weirdest thing. You'll never believe it. I was trying to sleep but I felt... feverish. And then I realized. I am head over heels in love with you! Isn't that funny? You were right in front of me all these years.

(Breanna is still chanting.)

PENNY: Look at me. *(Breanna stops chanting and looks at her. Penny opens the sheet.)* Come here. *(Breanna crosses to Penny, who wraps the sheet around them both, enveloping them. There is quiet romantic music. They slow dance. Breanna lays her head on Penny's shoulder.)* I need you, Breanna. I've always needed you. I just never knew it before.

(They continue to slow dance for a while. Penny kisses Breanna. It is soft at first, but gathers intensity. They sink to the ground in the sheet, in a heat of passion, as-- MUSIC STOPS. LIGHTS TO NORMAL AS... We are in Penny's bedroom. The two girls are in bed, restless.)

PENNY: Stop touching me. God!

BREANNA: I can't help it. Your bed is small.

PENNY: I need to sleep.

BREANNA: Well, so do I. Stop talking, why don't you?

PENNY: You stop talking.

BREANNA: Fine.

PENNY: God! *(It is quiet for a moment. Penny sits up.)* I can't sleep.

BREANNA: Me neither.

PENNY: Everything is so shitty lately.

BREANNA: I know. It's weird that things are going back to normal, little by little. Mark Temple told me that the boys are going to stand in front of AM/PM tonight until someone buys them beer. Just like before. Jeff was their friend! Also... If he's dead, and I'm not saying that he is, whoever did it... I mean, he'll probably do it again. And this person obviously likes boys so Mark and those guys are really just sitting ducks when you think about it.

PENNY: I can't let myself believe that. That everything will go back to normal. People can't accept this, just let it happen. We're talking about human life here. That has value, right? It's worth something, isn't it? *(Beat.)* I have nightmares all the time now. About fingers. Fingers inching up my leg and into me, digging through my insides. I give birth and the baby is just a finger. An over-sized bloody finger in a placenta.

BREANNA: I wish we could get out.

PENNY: Me too.

BREANNA: We could, really.

PENNY: How?

BREANNA: Maybe we could stay with my brother in Portland.

PENNY: Danny lives in a dorm. I don't think he'd take us in.

BREANNA: Maybe he would, just until we found jobs and a place to live.

PENNY: What kind of jobs could we get?

BREANNA: We could be like professional witches, casting spells for people and giving psychic readings. Like Sylvia Browne on *The Montel William Show*. Ooh... or we could work at Urban Outfitters!

PENNY: Be realistic. If we ran away we'd end up junkie hookers like in all those Lifetime movies.

BREANNA: Maybe. So I saw you and Trisha Sorensen again yesterday. Are you guys, like, friends now?

PENNY: I don't know. Kind of, I guess. I was thinking that she could join our coven.

BREANNA: Really? Do you think she has the gift?

PENNY: Not necessarily, but neither do you.

BREANNA: Yes, I do!

PENNY: No. You don't.

BREANNA: Whatever. That's cold.

PENNY: Anyway, I'm sick of only having one friend.

BREANNA: I thought I was your best friend.

PENNY: You are.

BREANNA: Look, I just don't think you should trust her so easily. She thrives on drama.

PENNY: We're just going shopping for baby clothes.

BREANNA: Just be careful. I've known her my whole life. Believe me, I'm just trying to protect you.

PENNY: I appreciate it. As annoying as it is sometimes, secretly I'm glad I have you to look after me.

BREANNA: *(Touching Penny's face, gently.)* You're my best friend and... I mean, I love you.

PENNY: I love you too. *(Breanna inches in and kisses Penny. Penny kisses her back for a moment. She wakes up to what is happening and breaks free.)* What the--

BREANNA: I'm sorry.

PENNY: Breanna, are you--

BREANNA: I don't know why I did that.

PENNY: Are you a lesbian?

BREANNA: Are you kidding? No way.

PENNY: Seriously, are you?

BREANNA: I already said that I wasn't.

PENNY: It's cool if you are. Seriously, Chad in my French class is gay and he's awesome.

BREANNA: I'm not a lesbian!

PENNY: Okay, okay!

BREANNA: At least... I don't think so. It's confusing.

PENNY: What's confusing about it? You're either a lezzy or you're not. Do you like boys or girls?

BREANNA: Neither. I don't like people. Like, at all. The more I think about it, the more I think people are just pretty unremarkable. When I was little my family went to Disney World and we saw this 3-D movie. I don't remember what it was about but I remember that Michael Jackson was in it. What I do remember is that feeling of seeing something new. Not something under the surface, but over it. I think most people aren't wearing their 3-D glasses, you know? They can't see all that extra stuff. And if a person *is* wearing their glasses it makes what other people see, like, really boring. I think... I think you're the only remarkable person I know.

PENNY: Breanna...

BREANNA: Does that make me gay? I mean, I do love you and everything.

PENNY: I don't know.

BREANNA: I don't know either.

(Breanna touches Penny's face again.)

PENNY: Please stop touching my face. It makes me really uncomfortable.

BREANNA: I'm sorry.

PENNY: Seriously, why do you keep doing that?

BREANNA: I just wanted to.

PENNY: Did Trisha say something to you?

BREANNA: No. I don't know.

PENNY: Because I said something to her and... oh, man. I'm gonna kick her ass!

BREANNA: No. I don't know what you're talking about, I really don't.

PENNY: Liar.

BREANNA: I promise.

PENNY: Then how do you know?

BREANNA: Let's just go back to sleep.

PENNY: Tell me!

BREANNA: All right. Fine. I watched you walking with Trisha yesterday and I followed you guys into the woods. I heard everything. I'm sorry.

PENNY: Bitch.

BREANNA: I'm sorry!

PENNY: Dyke!

BREANNA: Listen, Penny--

PENNY: --No, you listen. You took something private, an intimate secret I shared with Trisha, and you used it to make me be gay for you! What's wrong with you? Do you really think I would ever do that? With you? Just get out of here. God!

BREANNA: It's almost one in the morning.

PENNY: I don't care. I want you gone.

BREANNA: I understand that you're pissed off, I really do, but it's not safe out there.

PENNY: GET OUT.

(It is quiet, as if Breanna is trying to decide how to proceed. After a moment she crosses to exit.)

BREANNA: I really am sorry.

PENNY: You're gonna be even sorrier. I'm gonna tell everybody about tonight. I'm gonna tell them all you're a fat dyke. Now get out of my room!

(Breanna exits.)

PENNY: Fucking dyke.

(LIGHTS SHIFT AS... Penny exits as Trisha enters with binoculars. Crickets chirp as Trisha speaks to the audience, looking through her binoculars. During her speech we see Breanna appear in the shadows with her thumb out. She is hitch hiking.)

TRISHA: Yeah, so... that's Breanna Stark. Hitch hiking at 1:30 in the morning. In her pajamas. She might as well wear a sign around her neck that says "violate me". Then again, who would want to? *(Breanna disappears.)* In a town as small as this there is nothing good happening at 1:30 in the morning. Let's just check in with Clear Creek, shall we? Let's see what people are doing at the exact moment Breanna is hitch hiking. Fun! Penny Lauder is trying to fall asleep. Breanna doesn't know it yet, but her parents are still awake. Fighting. She'll sneak into the house but she won't need to. Her parents didn't even know she was gone. Miss Murkowski is also awake in her house on Ponderosa Street. She's been having nightmares, so she's having a glass of white wine and watching infomercials instead of sleeping. There are seventy-six people drinking by themselves in Clear Creek at this exact moment, though not all of them are shit faced. There are thirty-two men masturbating. One of them is John Stratton, who does like Penny Lauder and is fantasizing about her as he jerks it. It's funny how the sizes of their junk varies so much from body to body. This is something that will never cease to amaze me, I think. I'm not supposed to be thinking about stuff like this. I'm trying to have clean thoughts. But let's get serious. I'm not made of wood, people. Anyway, about seven or eight people get the shivers and the feeling like they are being watched. Guess what? Sometimes when you get the feeling you're being watched... it's because you're being watched. Just something to think about. Is this still Part Five? I lose track.

(LIGHTS SHIFT TO... Trisha has exited. At some point during her last speech two chairs have been set. A truck. Lauren is driving. She is wearing a ball cap and work shirt. Maybe she has a mustache? She has transformed into GILL, a middle-aged trucker.)

BREANNA: Thanks for the ride.

GILL: Young thing like you shouldn't be out this late. It's not right.

BREANNA: No, I know it's after curfew. I got into a fight with my girlfriend.

GILL: School night, isn't it?

BREANNA: Yeah.

GILL: Guess you probably heard about that kid.

BREANNA: He's in my class.

GILL: Not no more.

BREANNA: You don't know that.

GILL: Kid's mom got his finger in the mail. Boy ain't dead he's in a world of pain. Bet whoever did it would love a tasty bit like you.

BREANNA: It seems like whoever did it likes boys.

GILL: You mean he's some sort of homosexual?

BREANNA: I don't know.

GILL: Nah. Homo couldn't do that. You gotta have a stomach to cut somebody's finger off. You're probably too young to remember but there was a boy got killed six or seven years before this Chalk boy. You ever heard of Peter Calhoun?

BREANNA: Oh yeah. I'd forgotten about that.

GILL: Shouldn't forget about stuff like that. That's how people get away with it. There were kids before Peter too, you know. Goes back twenty-five years or so. Marcus Lister, they found his penis in the creek. And Dave Hooper was in the creek too, his face was--

BREANNA: --I don't want to know.

GILL: Guy must wait until people have forgotten. It's probably like Christmas for him. All that waiting, the anticipation, years and years, and then when the moment is right... SPLAT. He slices again.

BREANNA: I don't see how a person could do that.

GILL: I do.

BREANNA: You do?

GILL: It's about power. See, society's become really emasculating to us men. You got your women's rights, you black rights, your faggot's rights. What about us? Time was America was paradise for the white man. But that's been taken away, see?

BREANNA: That's ridiculous.

GILL: You think so? Blacks and spicks got all our honest jobs. Came right in and took 'em. Women are wearing the pants in the household. Man, they run huge corporations now. Can't call a faggot a faggot without somebody saying you're a bigot. Our power's been taken from us. My guess is the killer is a white man sick of being kicked around. He's obsessed with having power. Not just power over any old body, but power of the grand prize in his eyes. He gets off on having power over good looking, rich, young white males. A white boy is still the holy grail in this country.

BREANNA: What about white *girls*?

GILL: Good for a fuck but otherwise who gives a shit?

BREANNA: Charmed. This is my house. Right here.

GILL: Jesus. You live in a palace. You're one lucky girl. Bet your parents wouldn't be too happy to have you out hitching all hours.

BREANNA: No, I guess they wouldn't. Thanks for the ride.

GILL: Hey, a rich girl like you should try to fix herself up a bit. Could be a real knock out. You almost look like a boy in them clothes.

(Breanna gets out of the car, uncomfortable.)

BREANNA: Thanks again for the lift.

GILL: Name's Gill.

BREANNA: Thanks, Gill.

GILL: You're welcome, Missy. What's your name?

BREANNA: Beverly.

GILL: Pretty name. Be seeing you, Beverly.

(Breanna dashes off. LIGHTS SHIFT AS... Lauren removes the ball cap, mustache and work shirt. She becomes herself again and speaks to the audience. During the speech she is setting the stage for the scene that is to follow.)

LAUREN: I'm on the yearbook staff. It's just a fun thing to do after school, you know? Plus, it will look really good on my Stanford application. Also, and I sort of hate to admit this, I want the yearbook to be full of people I actually like. Anyway, when we were planning the layout of the yearbook this year our club advisor, Mrs. Bard, she said to leave two pages blank. She said don't plan them. She said it was because every year at least one student dies and you have to leave room for their memorial. Last year I guess Michelle Lichter died of a heart defect. She passed away in her sleep one week before her first formal. The year before that Fred Percy died in a car accident while he was drag racing. He'd been drinking and drove his car off Horse Shoe Ridge. He couldn't get his seatbelt off and so he drowned. This year... Well. Day twenty-three. *The* day. Part Six. The End.

(She writes this on the chalkboard and-- LIGHT SHIFT AND... Penny appears, at the doctor's office. She is in stirrups. Lauren transforms into Mom and marches up to her.)

MOM: You little turd.

PENNY: What?

MOM: You're not pregnant. Well?

PENNY: I am so pregnant. I know it. Why else would I be putting on all this weight? Why else would I be throwing up all the time?

MOM: You're putting on weight because you eat like a hog. You should have heard Doctor Salisbury...

(Trisha appears in a bubble of light. She wears a white coat and has a clipboard. She is DOCTOR SALISBURY.)

DOCTOR SALISBURY: Well, she's not pregnant which frankly astounds me. May I be frank, Mrs. Lauder? She's no virgin. Not by a mile. Seriously, she is really beat up down there. I'd consider therapy for the girl. *Blah blah blobbity blah...*

MOM: I asked about the vomiting...

DOCTOR SALISBURY: *(Shrugging.)* Irritable bowel syndrome? Have her poop in this cup and bring it back to.

(Doctor Salisbury disappears.)

MOM: Not being pregnant is good news, Penelope. Having babies is what women do to destroy their lives. Now you have a second chance! You can graduate and go to college and still have a family later if you want to.

PENNY: Get real. None of that will ever happen for me.

MOM: What am I gonna do with you? God knows I'm trying. I'm doing my best, but I feel as if I've lost touch with you. I see this person you've become and I don't recognize her. How many partners have you had?

PENNY: What?

MOM: Partners! How many sexual partners have you had?

PENNY: Just Jeff.

MOM: I don't believe you.

PENNY: I'm not lying!

MOM: Tell me.

PENNY: I don't know!

MOM: You don't know?

PENNY: No, I don't know. Are you satisfied?

MOM: Five? More than five?

PENNY: I don't know. Yes.

MOM: Oh lord. Penny, what is going on? Do you want to talk to a professional?

PENNY: No.

MOM: Well, then talk to me.

PENNY: Do you regret having me?

MOM: Sometimes.

PENNY: That's awesome.

MOM: Well, what do you want me to say? Raising children is the hardest job in the world, especially by yourself.

PENNY: I'll never regret having my baby. Not ever.

MOM: Penny, you aren't pregnant.

PENNY: Yes, I am.

MOM: I just don't understand you. Listen, Penelope. This is the best thing that could have happened. God, sometimes I wish that you were gay like your little friend. Men. They're the worst.

PENNY: Breanna is gay, by the way. She came onto me last night.

MOM: Did you two--

PENNY: No! Just because Breanna is gay doesn't mean I am.

MOM: I think you should try it.

PENNY: What? God!

MOM: I'm telling you now, nobody will ever treat you as good as Breanna does. These boys, when they're gone Breanna will still be there by your side.

PENNY: Stop talking.

MOM: Just try it! God, I'd never have to worry about you—

PENNY: Stop it! God!

MOM: All right, all right. Come on. Let's go.

PENNY: Where?

MOM: I have to take you back to school.

PENNY: Can't I go home?

MOM: I think it's important to move on, don't you? Now that this mess is behind us?

PENNY: I don't want to move on. I wanna watch MTV and eat ice cream.

MOM: Why are you lying? About being pregnant?

PENNY: I'm not.

MOM: I just don't understand.

PENNY: Can't you see that I'm lucky? I'm going to be the mother to the most amazing guy's baby. And when Jeff is back we'll be together. We'll be a real family.

MOM: I wish I could tell you that you didn't have to lie. That you didn't have to manipulate people to make them stay with you.

PENNY: I know, mom.

MOM: I love you, Penny.

PENNY: I love you too.

MOM: Okay, then. Let's go.

(They exit as-- LIGHTS SHIFT AND... A school bell rings as all four girls enter and sit in their chairs, arranging a classroom. Penny and Trisha sit next to one another. Lauren and Breanna are far off to either side.)

BREANNA: Psst... Penny.

TRISHA: Fuck off, pig dyke whore.

BREANNA: I have to talk to you. Meet me behind the football field after school, okay?

TRISHA: She doesn't want to talk to you.

LAUREN: Will you guys please be quiet? I don't want to get in trouble.

TRISHA: She told me you tried to finger her last night. That's disgusting Breanna Stark, and a sin. We both hate you.

BREANNA: You're the disgusting one, Trisha. *(The following rises until she is yelling.)* Your voice, your face, your hair, your black little soul, are all disgusting. I am not a pig or a dyke or a whore. I'm gay. Yeah, I'm gay, but so what? You're the most unlikable person ever. Everybody who has ever met you hates you. Try and figure out why, bitch—

LAUREN: --Seriously, be quiet.

BREANNA: Now if you don't shut up and mind your own business I will kick you so hard in your puffy vagina that you granddaughters will be STERILE.

TRISHA: That's it. I'm telling Miss Murkowski!

76

BREANNA: Go ahead! She hates you too! *(Trisha runs off into the shadows and Breanna sits next to Penny.)* Penny, you have to talk to me.

PENNY: I don't have anything to say.

BREANNA: I understand why you're upset, I really do--

PENNY: No, I'm not mad. I just, I don't know, I think it's easier to be alone right now is all.

BREANNA: Alone? What about Trisha?

PENNY: It's the next best thing. I can't even hear her when she talks anymore. Even when it's not about jeans, it just sounds like white noise.

LAUREN: That's mean, Penny.

PENNY: Mind your own business!

BREANNA: I'm sorry that I tried to manipulate you. I just can't stand not being near you all the time.

PENNY: Leave me alone.

(Trisha, as Miss Murkowski, reenters from the shadows. She holds a crumpled tissue and occasionally blows her nose into it. She is crying.)

MISS MURKOWSKI: Okey-dokey, class. I have an announcement. Eyes on me. Eyes here. I hate to be the bearer of bad news. Such an awful thing has happened. This morning the police recovered Jeffrey Chalk's body from the creek. It was weighted down and had been there for some time. It's so awful... *(She goes into a crying fit as her words devolve into gibberish.)* Blah blah blobbity-blah blah blah. The children are our future blobbity- blah. Each life is precious blobbity-blah blah blah. OH GOD! *(During this, Penny locks eyes with Breanna and then dashes from the room.)* Penelope! Where are you going? *(Breanna decides to follow her and dashes out behind her.)* Breanna Stark, get back here! Please? Girls. Don't leave me here all alone! *(She is hysterical. Lauren crosses to her.)*

LAUREN: It's going to be okay, Miss Murkowski.

(Lauren puts her arm around Miss Murkowski, comforting her.)

MISS MURKOWSKI: Nothing is ever going to be okay. Oh God! I'm going to die!

LAUREN: No, you're not. Shh...

MISS MURKOWSKI: I am so!

LAUREN: No, none of that. Quiet, Miss Murkowski...

MISS MURKOWSKI: Will you call me by my first name?

LAUREN: Uh. Okay.

MISS MURKOWSKI: It's Beth!

LAUREN: Everything is going to be okay, Beth. Come on. Let's pray together. *(They kneel and hold hands.)* Our father, who art in heaven... Come on you know this, Beth.

(They begin to pray together.)

MISS MURKOWSKI & LAUREN: Our father who art in heaven, hallowed be thy name. Thy kingdom come, thy will be done on Earth as it is in heaven...

(The light changes strangely as they pray. Penny appears on another part of the stage. She is down by the creek, which is now a world of water and police tape. She is drawing a pentagram in the dirt with the sacred dagger.)

MISS MURKOWSKI & LAUREN: Give us this day our daily bread. And forgive us our trespasses as we forgive those that trespass against us. And lead us not into temptation, but deliver us from evil: for thine is the kingdom, and the power, and the glory, forever. Amen.

(They embrace for a moment and then exit as... LIGHTS FINISH SHIFTING AND... We are down by the creek at night. Penelope is lighting candles and placing them at the points of the pentagram. Breanna enters with a flashlight and watches her.)

BREANNA: I followed you. Don't be mad. So is this where they found him?

PENNY: Down there some.

BREANNA: I'm so sorry.

PENNY: Do you believe that a person can be born unlucky?

BREANNA: I think maybe we make our own luck.

PENNY: I think I was, maybe. Look what other people have, what you have, or what Lauren Radley has, or anybody for that matter. Clean houses and families that care and clean skin and nice jeans. How come I didn't get any of that? It's not fair.

BREANNA: Nobody ever said life was fair.

PENNY: Yes, they did. They said it constantly, the fucking liars.

BREANNA: Who?

PENNY: Them. Grown-ups... that we were each special or whatever? It's such bullshit. Only some people matter, only some people are special, and that's just the way it is. The truth is that everybody ends up exactly where they started no matter what. Do not pass go. Do not collect two hundred dollars.

BREANNA: I don't know. I think--

PENNY: I think that's why I started casting spells. I thought I could, I don't know, level the playing field a little. Too bad it doesn't work. I'm a fraud.

BREANNA: We both wanted it to be true. The power, I mean. If we're not powerful witches then we're only two stupid fucking kids, right?

PENNY: That's us.

BREANNA: I don't know. When Trisha stopped talking to me I thought it was, like, the end. I had nobody and I'd lie in the dark listening to boo-hoo crybaby music non-stop. I would lie in the dark and wish I wasn't so lonely. And then, finally, there was you. So, I don't know, I think we make our own luck. Maybe wishing hard enough is a sort of spell.

PENNY: Do you think Jeff was in love with me?

BREANNA: It's nice to think so. But I love you and your mom does too and there's gonna be a lot of people who love you. Including your kid, I mean, that's huge, right?

PENNY: A baby. God! How am I gonna raise a baby?

BREANNA: With help. Lots and lots of help. Me, your mom, Trisha even.

PENNY: I don't want Trisha near my kid. She seems like she might be a baby shaker. Shit. I feel like I'm twenty-five years old. God!

BREANNA: I'm tired too. Are you hungry? We should go to Taco Bell. Come on, I'll buy you a chulupa.

PENNY: No, I wanna try the spell again.

BREANNA: Yeah? Okay then.

(Lauren enters, with Trisha behind her. They both have flashlights.)

LAUREN: Hey.

BREANNA: Leave us alone.

TRISHA: Look, we didn't come here to fight.

BREANNA: Great. You can go now.

LAUREN: What are you guys doing?

PENNY: Nothing.

LAUREN: You're doing a spell, aren't you? You're going to try to contact him.

PENNY: Yeah.

TRISHA: That's awesome. I want to help.

BREANNA: No.

LAUREN: Trisha, don't. It's a sin.

TRISHA: I can't be perfect all the time, Lauren. Don't you get sick of always trying to be perfect? You loved Jeff, right? Well, now you might be able to tell him.

BREANNA: No, no, no.

TRISHA: Oh, come on, Breanna.

PENNY: *(To Breanna.)* It could help to have four.

BREANNA: Fine. *(To Lauren and Trisha.)* But you have to be serious and do what we say.

TRISHA: Fine.

PENNY: Okay. Get in the circle. *(Trisha joins Penny and Breanna in the circle. They look to Lauren.)* Are you in or not?

LAUREN: Okay. I'm in.

(Lauren enters the circle and the ritual begins. Penny holds a dagger in front of her heart, then lifts it above her head.)

PENNY: I call upon the Watchtowers of the North. I call upon the goddess and the horned god.

(She passes the dagger to Breanna, who repeats the motions.)

BREANNA: I call upon the Watchtowers of the South. I call upon the goddess and the horned god. *(Breanna passes the dagger to Trisha. She leads her in what to say.)* The East...

TRISHA: I call upon the Watchtowers of the East.

BREANNA: The goddess and the horned god...

TRISHA: I call upon the goddess and the horned god.

(Trisha passes the dagger to Lauren, who repeats the motion.)

LAUREN: I call upon the watchtowers of the West. I call upon the goddess and the horned god.

(Penny lays out the purple cloth.)

PENNY: Protect us from harm.

BREANNA: Protect us from harm.

PENNY: Protect us from harm.

ALL: Protect us from harm.

(Penny lights a black candle.)

PENNY: Visit us, spirits. Bless us with your patronage. With this candle we invoke thee...

ALL: With this candle we invoke thee.

(The metal bowl of garlic is placed out.)

PENNY: Receive our offering.

ALL: Receive our offering.

(The wine is in the goblet and each girl in turn pricks her finger with a needle and squeezes the blood into it.)

PENNY: Everyone join hands. *(The girls link hands.)* We call forth the spirit of Jeff Chalk. You have left this mortal coil and may enter our circle. Let us be your mouth. Speak through we women, Jeff Chalk! So mote it be!

BREANNA: So mote it be!

ALL: So mote it be! So mote it be! SO MOTE IT BE!

(Suddenly the light is blinding white and everything is deadly quiet. The four girls are frozen until Penny timidly steps out of the circle and approaches the audience.)

PENNY: Sorry I've been ignoring you. It's just that I'm not one of the narrators so I'm supposed to act like you're not here. Anyway, I wanted to tell you my version of what happened next, because I know that they'll leave it out. We're doing the spell when there is a blinding light. All is white and time stands still. It's day. It was night a moment ago and now it's day and the whole class is here at the creek. *(The sounds of water and laughing as the frozen girls begin to move.)* Everyone is being so nice to each other. Mark Temple just did a belly flop off the dock. Ashley has on the world's littlest bikini. Miss Murkowski is eating a tuna sandwich. She drops it on the ground but eats it anyway, not knowing she was seen. Ten second rule. It's weird, but my mom is here. She waves. I feel a perfect contentment. Is that a word? Contentment? And then-- then there's Jeff Chalk. *(Somehow Trisha has transformed into Jeff Chalk. Jeff Chalk moves slowly toward Penny.)* He comes up out of the water, his hair is matted to the sides of his face. He's an image from *Men's Fitness* and he's coming right toward me. I could die right now, I think, and I'll be happy. He comes over to where I'm sitting in the grass. *(Jeff Chalk crosses to Penny and kneels before her.)* He kneels down in front of me and puts his hand on my cheek. Nice and gentle. *(He does.)* Then, the best part. He kisses me softly. An innocent kiss. *(Jeff Chalk kisses Penny.)* And he leans into me and he whispers--

LAUREN: I.

BREANNA: Am.

PENNY: Totally

LAUREN: Not.

ALL: Gone.

(Trisha turns back and the girls begin to go back to the spots wherein they were frozen.)

PENNY: I saw this happen as clear as day. I'm not delusional or crazy. Jeff came to me and he spoke to me, comforted me when I needed it, and it was magic. You think I'd lie to you?

(The lights return to normal and the girls unfreeze, finishing their spell.)

ALL: So mote it be! So mote it be! SO MOTE IT BE!

(It is quiet for a moment as the girls try to assess whether anything happened.)

LAUREN: What happened?

PENNY: I don't know.

BREANNA: Does anybody notice anything different?

TRISHA: No.

LAUREN: It didn't work.

BREANNA: Maybe it did.

LAUREN: It didn't fucking work.

TRISHA: Lauren...

LAUREN: Shut up, Trisha.

TRISHA: You shut up!

PENNY: Both of you shut up. Jeff was just here. You didn't--

BREANNA: What are you talking about?

PENNY: Didn't you feel it? It was like time froze and Jeff spoke. Jeff spoke to me.

TRISHA: I know, right? It was so weird.

BREANNA: I guess I felt a little weird.

PENNY: I mean, he came right up to me and he said that even though he passed on he's not totally gone, you know, and that he loves me and he's watching over me and the baby.

TRISHA: Wow.

LAUREN: Just shut up.

PENNY: Just because you can't--

LAUREN: Stop pretending!

BREANNA: This isn't a game, Lauren--

LAUREN: --I know it's not a game! Okay? Jeff Chalk is dead.

TRISHA: He's in heaven now.

LAUREN: You don't believe that. Not really. The truth is that when Jeff was killed he just blinked out. Like an old light bulb. Somebody did that to him. You know? Took his life? It makes me think the idea of predestination is pretty fucking idiotic. I mean, who is predestined for torture and sexual abuse and murder?

BREANNA: Don't be ignorant.

LAUREN: I mean, we have to stop pretending here. My faith, it was... I can't reconcile my intelligence with what's not based in the, I don't know, the obvious. The facts. What you see is what you get. Plain and simple. There is only this. No order, no magic, no reason, no mystery, no logic, no god. *(She focuses her attention to Penny.)* I loved him. Did you know that? As much as you. I really hate you for doing those things with Jeff. I mean, I really do. It makes me sick to think about--

PENNY: --Leave me alone.

LAUREN: You're worth absolutely nothing at all.

BREANNA: Come on...

LAUREN: Nothing. Jeff Chalk, he was special, you know? When Murkowski announced he'd died I thought, good. Now he belongs to everybody. But you know what? I see that he doesn't belong to anybody. Jeff Chalk is dead, plain and simple.

PENNY: I hate you.

LAUREN: Gone.

PENNY: Shut up.

LAUREN: Finished.

(Penny lunges at her with the dagger. Chaos. Yelling. Penny has Lauren pinned.)

TRISHA: Oh my god!

BREANNA: Penny!

LAUREN: Go ahead. Do it.

(Penny drags the knife against Lauren's cheek, cutting it. Lauren screams. Penny releases her.)

PENNY: You think you're worth so much? There. You're worth a little less now.

TRISHA: You're insane! Are you all right, Lauren?

LAUREN: You'll regret that.

PENNY: I don't regret.

(Trisha huddles around Lauren.)

TRISHA: Let's get you to a doctor.

(Trisha begins to pull Lauren into the shadows. Lauren looks back to tell Penny something.)

LAUREN: Seriously. If there's a God, he isn't watching.

(Trisha and Lauren are gone.)

BREANNA: You shouldn't have done that.

PENNY: Fuck.

BREANNA: What should we do?

PENNY: Fuck. Fuck. Fuck.

BREANNA: Well...

PENNY: What if she's right? What if this is it?

BREANNA: She's not right.

PENNY: Well, what if she is?

BREANNA: Would it be so bad? I mean, is your life that bad? So many people love you. Your mom. Me. The baby. Isn't that enough?

(Penny looks at Breanna.)

PENNY: No. It isn't enough.

BREANNA: We'll make it enough. I know we can. I mean, we can make a real family.

PENNY: If Lauren is right, if nothing ever happens for a reason, then I can do whatever I want. I mean, it's kind of a gift, really.

BREANNA: What does that mean?

PENNY: Let's make a family.

BREANNA: Really?

PENNY: Let's do it.

(Breanna is exuberant. She holds Penny.)

BREANNA: I can't believe we're having a baby.

PENNY: Yeah. We're having a baby. Just stay with me, Breanna. Okay? Don't ever let me go.

BREANNA: No. Not ever.

(They exit arm in arm as-- LIGHTS SHIFT TO: Lauren and Trisha are in their positions from the top of Act One. Lauren writes "epilogue" on the chalkboard. They speak to the audience.)

LAUREN: Hi.

TRISHA: Hello. How are you holding up? You okay?

LAUREN: In case you were wondering, the answer is yes. I will always have a scar on my cheek.

TRISHA: It looks okay.

LAUREN: Thanks. That's weird...

TRISHA: What?

LAUREN: I can see the future so clearly from here.

TRISHA: Really? So what happens?

LAUREN: *(As if just skimming a passage in an article.)* Stanford. Marry my college sweetheart. Move to Philadelphia where I work as an attorney. Have daughter. Daughter dies at age nine. Leukemia. Husband leaves. I make partner. Trisha?

TRISHA: State school, then back to Clear Creek. Work in real estate. Marry Mark Temple, how about that? Four children, all girls. I stop working. My family is big but I'm overwhelmingly lonely sometimes. Have affair after affair. Work things out with Mark. Oh... and more kids disappear in Clear Creek. All boys.

LAUREN: Yikes. Those are just the short versions. I guess neither of us know what happens to Penny or Breanna. Do you, Trisha?

TRISHA: I saw Penny from time to time, but after high school... nothing.

LAUREN: Guess they really didn't matter.

TRISHA: Let's just ask them. Hey, Breanna...*(Breanna appears.)* What happens to you? Are you happy in the future?

BREANNA: Uh... Smith College. Lots of beer. Lots of girls. Backpack though Europe after graduation. Settle in Portland, Oregon. Work with at-risk youth, ironically. My partner and I have a baby. Raise her. It's a nice quiet life. And I'm happy.

TRISHA: Congratulations.

BREANNA: Thank you.

(Breanna disappears.)

LAUREN: You go now, Penny.

(Penny appears.)

PENNY: What?

LAUREN: What happens to you?

PENNY: I don't want to say.

LAUREN: Oh, come on.

PENNY: No. It doesn't matter. It's not relevant and whatever your assumptions are, they're probably true. Things don't always work out the way we hope they will. I don't live in Clear Creek, but I think about it sometimes. I think about all of you and I wonder what you're doing. Mostly though I think about Jeff.

TRISHA: Hmm.

PENNY: Can I go?

TRISHA: It's a free country, isn't it?

(Penny disappears. Lauren and Trisha begin cleaning up.)

LAUREN: Well, there you have it, folks.

TRISHA: That's all she wrote.

LAUREN: Life only moves forward.

TRISHA: You know, I see many more Taco Bells in Clear Creek's future. Pizza Huts too. It's very convenient.

LAUREN: That's how we all get fat.

TRISHA: Our place by the creek gets turned into a parking lot!

LAUREN: Go figure. Clear Creek is like every small town. All along the highways they look exactly the same, forming a dotted line across the grotesque belly of America.

TRISHA: That's beautiful.

LAUREN: It shows the blade where to cut. Where to release the blood and fat. It's the same all over. In the end, nothing about us matters. It's all forgotten. Anyway, enjoy the complimentary Orangeade on your way out.

TRISHA: I made it.

LAUREN: Okay. Bye.

TRISHA: Kisses, bitches.

(They begin to erase the chalk boards as lights go down.)

END OF PLAY.

OWL MOON
By Liz Maestri

Synopsis: What happens when an Owl Moon rises? The everyday world veers into extremities – hot blood spurts and passions seep into a wintry landscape of cold and desolation. Two couples venture into a desolate, frozen snowfield for the night where they find themselves trapped, both physically and in the mire of their own neurosis. Lisa is determined to win back her ex, Isaac, and will stop at nothing to do so. Shell and Salome carry weighty sacks across the snow, looking for a way to purge their sins. The play follows this group of characters through conflicts and collisions that stretch taut conventions of style and tone. Is it possible to lose oneself? To lose oneself in another? Owl Moon examines the fine line between passion and obsession, and the toll it takes on the mind and spirit. Add in a talking owl, and you have a play that juggles the heady, humorous and harrowing in equal measure.

Cast Size: 1 Male, 3 Females, 1 Talking Owl

MITZI'S ABORTION by Elizabeth Heffron

Synopsis: With humor, intelligence and honesty, "Mitzi's Abortion" explores the questions that have shaped the national debate over abortion, and reminds us that whatever we may think we believe, some decisions are neither easy nor simple when they become ours to make. A generous and compassionate comedy with serious themes about a young woman trying to make an intensely personal decision in a system determined to make it a political one.

Cast Size: 3 Females, 4 Males

R & J & Z by Melody Bates

Synopsis: What if Romeo and Juliet got a second chance? "R & J & Z" begins with Act V of Shakespeare's Romeo and Juliet and keeps going, as the famous lovers navigate a world in which death isn't necessarily the end. Set against the historical backdrop of Verona's plague, Melody Bates' new verse play throws old and new characters together over the course of an apocalyptic and action-packed 24 hours. Equally inspired by Shakespeare and modern zombie films, "R & J & Z" pushes the boundaries of theatrical humor and horror.

Cast Size: Diverse Cast of 15-19

<u>LITTLE MAN</u> by Bekah Brunstetter

Synopsis: Howie has spent the last decade trying to forget the traumas of high school. But when an invitation to his ten year reunion arrives, he hops on a plane home to discover just what happened to the jocks, the prom queens, and the social outcasts- and whether anyone cares that he's a millionaire now. With wry wit and penetrating insight, Bekah Brunstetter's heartbreaking comedy takes us on a hilariously awkward and unexpectedly moving journey in which no one can completely abandon who they used to be.

Cast Size: 3 Males, 3 Females

WHERE ALL GOOD RABBITS GO
by Karina Cochran

Synopsis: During the Age of the Rabbit, no one died. That is to say no one died in the typical way we now view death (the mystical removal of life from the body). Instead people became rabbits. This could happen very suddenly, or gradually over a long period of time. But sooner or later everyone became a rabbit. When hard working young farmer Walter suddenly sprouts a fluffy tail, his journey to where all good rabbits go begins, and there is no turning back.

Cast Size: 1 Female, 2 Males, 5 Chorus

NOTES

NOTES

Made in the USA
Monee, IL
19 May 2023

34102580R00056